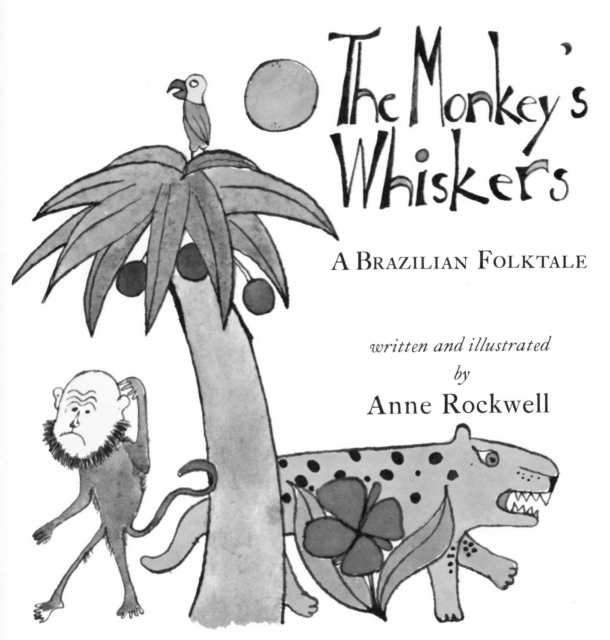

The Monkey's Whiskers

A Brazilian Folktale

written and illustrated
by

Anne Rockwell

Parents' Magazine Press : New York

THE MONKEY'S WHISKERS is but one segment, freely adapted, from a long and involved story which appeared first in Andrew Lang's BROWN FAIRY BOOK. This in turn had been translated from a story in FOLKLORE BRASILIEN. Because of the basically European structure of the story, plus a reference to elephants in one of the other sequences of the tale, it quite likely originated in Portugal. The Brazilian aspects have been emphasized, however, and include a coffee picker as well as featuring South American birds in the pictures.

for
Hannah, Elizabeth
& Oliver

his is the place where the coconut trees grow taller and the parrots call noisier and the flowers are redder than anywhere else in the world.

High in the tallest coconut palm, a monkey lived.
He passed his days full of mischief, swinging from
tree to tree by his wonderful tail, and dropping coconuts on the jaguars who tiptoed below and the alligators who swam in the river.

One day the monkey decided to swing down from
the trees and see the world.

Past a bend in the river stood a little town, and in the town there was a barbershop. Looking inside, the monkey saw the barber shaving a man, and he wondered how *he* would look without his whiskers. He hopped into the barber chair and demanded that the barber shave his whiskers, and quickly at that. Although he had never before shaved a monkey, the barber did.

When he was finished, the monkey looked into the mirror. At first he said nothing. But then he began to jump up and down in the barber chair, squealing angrily, "Where are my whiskers? I want them back!"

Patiently and politely the barber tried to explain that the whiskers could not be put back. The more he explained, the angrier the monkey became, until at last he said, "Then give me your razor. I must take that if you will not give me back my whiskers which you have taken away!"

So the barber gave the monkey his razor, although he was sad to do so, for it was the shiniest and sharpest one he had.

The monkey walked on through the town, carrying the razor. He was still grumbling to himself about his lost whiskers when he came to a woman who was cleaning a fish at the river's edge. Because she was poor, she had only a scrap of wood to scrape off the fish scales.

"Here," said the monkey, pretending to be very kind and polite, "take my razor. You will be able to clean and scale your fish very quickly with it."

And before the woman even had a chance to say thank you, he scampered away to see more of the town.

Later on he returned to the woman and said to her, "Give me back my razor now."

But the woman sighed and said, "Ahhh! It was slippery in the water and it slid out of my hand. I am afraid that the river has carried it away."

"What! You have lost my beautiful razor!" The monkey's teeth chattered with anger and he shouted, "Then you must give me your fish!"

And plead as she would for all her hungry little children who would have no supper that night, the monkey would hear none of it. He insisted that she must give him the fish in return for the razor. Before long she did, and off he went, carrying the fresh fish that the woman had just baked.

Soon he came to a man sitting in the shade of a
coffee tree, munching on a piece of bread. It was yes-
terday's bread, dry and stale, but the man had no
water with which to wash it down.

"Here," said the monkey, sounding very kind and
polite, "that bread looks dry and tasteless. Take my
fish . . . you are welcome to it."

Thanking the monkey very much, the man ac-
cepted the fish. And the monkey scampered off to
see more of the town.

Next day the monkey came back to the man, who was picking coffee beans from the tree.

"Good morning," said the monkey. "I have come for my fish."

"Your fish!" cried the man. "Why I ate it last night for dinner."

"What! You have eaten the fish I loaned you?" shouted the monkey, jumping up and down in anger. "Then give me your coffee beans!" No sooner had the man given them to him than he was off.

He met a woman who was grinding flour outside her house.

"That flour will make a tasty cake," said the monkey, chuckling, "but don't you need some coffee to go with it?" And pretending to be very polite and friendly, he held out the little basket of coffee beans.

"Thank you!" said the woman, although she was surprised to see such a generous monkey.

The woman roasted the coffee beans, brewed them, and called her neighbors in. They drank up all the coffee. The monkey returned just as they were finishing the last drops.

"Give me back my coffee beans. I want them now myself," said the monkey, snarling grouchily.

"Ahhhhhh! That is not possible," said the woman. "We have used them all up."

"What!" screamed the monkey. "Used them up! I want my coffee beans back! I *must* have my coffee beans back!"

The monkey and the woman argued noisily back and forth. Then the monkey glanced toward the woman's stove. There stood a dish of the flour she had ground, for the cake she had baked had been a tiny one.

He said, "Well then, since you have taken my coffee beans, I will take your flour!"

He went down the road, carrying the dish of flour.
Before long he met a woman and her four pretty
little daughters sitting in the shade of a banana tree.
The woman was braiding the little girls' black and
shiny hair.

"My, what pretty little girls you have," said the monkey, sounding very kind and polite.

The woman smiled shyly, for she loved to hear her children praised, and to tell the truth, they were all beautiful.

"They look to be such sweet children," continued the monkey, "that they should have a cake for lunch. I have here some fresh-ground flour, and perhaps if you added a little coconut milk you could make a cake as sweet as they are."

At this the woman and all the little girls thanked the monkey, although they were surprised, for they were not accustomed to seeing such a polite and gentle monkey.

Next day the monkey came back.

"The cake was delicious!" said all the little girls.

"Thank you very much."

"Don't tell me," squealed the monkey, snarling and showing his teeth, "that you naughty children have eaten my flour!"

And the little girls admitted they had and began to cry.

"But," said their mother, "you gave us the flour for a cake, and we have used it all up."

"I didn't *give* it to you!" yelled the monkey, "I *loaned* it to you. But it does not matter; since you have used up what did not belong to you, I shall take something of yours. I would like a little girl to bake coconut cakes for me. I'll take *her*!" And he pointed to the woman's youngest and prettiest little girl.

The mother began to cry, and begged the monkey
on her hands and knees not to take her little girl away,
but the monkey would not listen to her.

All afternoon they argued, until the sun was nearly set. Still they argued, and would be arguing still had not the woman's husband come home from his work.

Now the husband was the same barber who had shaved the monkey's whiskers.

"Good evening," he said to the monkey. "Have you found my razor useful?"

Then the monkey began to shout at him. "So it's
you! If you had not taken away my beautiful whiskers,
I would not be taking your daughter!"

The barber looked at his wife, who was sobbing away. Then he looked at his pretty little girls, smiled a secret smile to himself, and said to the monkey, "If I could give you back your whiskers, then would you let us keep our little girl?"

The monkey frowned and thought for a moment. Then he growled a surly "yes," for to tell the truth, he was growing tired of the town. He was eager to get back to his home in the tall coconut palm, where he could drop coconuts on the jaguars tiptoeing below.

"Very well," said the barber. "It will be difficult, but I can do it. It will take eight days. Come with me." He led the monkey to a dark place underneath the house.

"You must stay here and sit perfectly still," said
the barber. "I shall give you a magic coconut to eat,
and I will cast a magic spell, and your whiskers will
come back to you. Mind you, I don't do this for
every customer. However, yours is a special case."

So the monkey stayed hidden under the house, where it was dark and cool, for eight whole days. He had never sat still for so long.

At the end of the eighth day, the barber came and called him out.

"Behold . . ." he said, "I gave you back your whiskers!" And he held up a mirror for the monkey to see. There were his whiskers, redder and fuzzier than ever before.

Joyously the monkey swung from tree to tree in
the barber's garden, and the barber and his wife and
little girls danced for joy.

All except the youngest and prettiest one, for *she* had thought it might be fun to learn to swing from tree to tree and learn all the tricks that monkeys know.

Suddenly the barber turned around, grew stern in the face, and shook his finger at the monkey. "Now," he said, "give me back my razor. I have returned your whiskers to you!"

When he heard this, the monkey swung by his tail
—again and again, from tree to tree, right out of town.
Back he went to the forest, where the coconut trees
grow taller and the parrots call noisier and the flowers
are redder than anywhere else in the world.

And he lives there still. He never came back to town, but keeps busy dropping coconuts down on the jaguars and alligators below.

And the barber and his wife and their pretty little
girls laugh, when they think of how the barber returned the monkey's whiskers to him.